Cover Design and Illustrations: Herb Heidinger

International Standard Book Number: 0-87879-316-X

1 0 9 8 7 6
0 9 8 7 6 5 4 3

You'll enjoy all the High Noon Books.
Write for a free full list of titles.

Contents

Chapter 1

Trouble on the Road

It was a late afternoon in August. Randy Flynn looked in his rear-view mirror. The car was still right behind him. He pressed the gas pedal to the floorboard. His black pick-up pulled ahead of the grey sedan. Now Randy turned the wheel sharply for a curve. There was a turn-around near the top of the mountain. He'd stop there and let that tail-gating jerk get ahead of him. His tires screeched as he braked for a hairpin turn. He looked in the mirror again. There it was. Close behind him. It followed him like a grey shadow.

Randy flicked on his turn signals for the turn-off. His hands were sweaty on the wheel. Dust rose as his truck bumped to a stop. The grey sedan roared by.

Randy climbed out of the truck. His legs felt shaky. Why did he feel a cold fear in the pit of

1

his stomach? Was it the car that had followed so close for the last ten miles? Or was it coming home for the first time in three years? He reached inside the glove compartment and took out a rag. Quickly he wiped the dust from the pick-up and its chrome wheels. He wanted his mother and sister to see his truck, the Shiny

Randy climbed out of the truck. His legs felt shaky.

Knight, at its best. It was only six months old. He took very good care of it. He stood back and looked at the truck. There! That was better. He tossed the rag back into the glove compartment.

Now he looked down into the valley. There was the water tower with CALVERTON painted in big black letters. Calverton—his home town. He could see the high school with its red tile roof. He'd had lots of good times there. And there was the town swimming pool. It took up almost a whole block. He thought about his days on the swimming team. Lots of memories.

At one time they had been good memories. But now they were just memories of a place where people thought his father was a thief. He swallowed hard. The lump in his throat tasted bitter. Calverton. Now it was just another place on the map. Except, of course, for Mom and Sis. Gosh, it would be good to see them.

Then he saw a brown pheasant chucking gravel on the side of the road. The bird bobbed its green head back and forth. Randy stayed very quiet. More memories crowded his head. The fun of hunting with his father. Sometimes they had hunted with Bill Markham, a trapper. If their luck wasn't good, it didn't matter. Just seeing the beautiful birds and being in the woods with Dad and Bill Markham was great.

Bill Markham. Then Randy remembered the letter. He took it from inside his leather jacket. He had read it many times. He read it again.

Dear Randy,
Sure miss your Dad. I guess you do, too. That is why I am writing. Saw something back in the mountains. Please come to Calvertoon SOON.

Your friend, Bill

Randy climbed back into his pick-up. Bill's letter made him want to hurry. He started the engine and shifted the truck into gear. The big tires spit out gravel as he pulled into the two-lane road.

As he drove down the mountain, his thoughts drifted to the past. Four years ago, his father, Jim Flynn, had been the assistant manager at Calverton State Bank. One Friday afternoon he left the bank early. He went to the airport and flew off in the bank's plane. That was it. Neither he nor the small plane was ever seen again.

Randy and his mother and sister had been stunned. It just didn't make sense. Then little bits of evidence began to turn up. First, Phil Stoner, a teller at the bank, had found an I.O.U. in Jim

Flynn's desk. It was made out to a gambling club in Reno. It was for $50,000. A few days later, Ike Harper, the bank president called the police. Fifty thousand dollars was missing from the bank.

It all seemed to add up. And Jim Flynn had been called a thief. Some people thought he had died in a plane crash. Others thought he had left the country with the money. Randy didn't know what to think. He didn't know if his dad was alive or dead. But he did know one thing. Jim Flynn was not a thief.

Now, just maybe, Bill Markham had seen something in the woods. Something that would prove Jim Flynn innocent.

Suddenly, out of the corner of his eye, Randy saw it. The grey sedan parked on the edge of the road. In a flash it raced onto the highway. Randy swerved to miss being hit broadside. Now the grey car was close behind him. It edged closer and closer.

Criminy! That idiot is going to hit me, Randy thought.

Chapter 2

Ski Mask

Randy stepped on the gas. But not soon enough. He heard the scraping sound as the sedan's bumper smashed into his rear bumper. He floored the accelerator. His truck laid a patch of rubber as it zoomed ahead. He looked in his rear-view mirror. The grey car was at least 25 yards behind him now.

Randy didn't slow down. His idea of fun wasn't playing "bumper tag" on a mountain road. And definitely not with someone wearing a brown ski mask! His knuckles were white where he gripped the steering wheel. He was sweating. "Come on, Shiny Knight, do your stuff," he said.

Slowly the distance between Randy's pick-up and the sedan grew wider. But he didn't slow down until he hit the 25-mile an hour zone in Calverton.

He hung a right onto Elm Street and drove two

blocks. He parked the pick-up in front of a low yellow house and got out.

"Randy!" a young girl yelled. The screen door slammed behind her.

"Hey, you're not the kid sister any more. You're all grown up." Randy hugged her tight. Then he saw his mother. All three hugged one another.

"Randy, it's so good to have you home. Come on in the house. I baked your favorite angel food cake," his mother said.

Randy grinned at her. "Somehow I knew there would be an angel food cake waiting. Some things never change, Mom."

When they were seated at the kitchen table with cake and milk, Mrs. Flynn asked, "Is everything all right, Randy? Did things go well at school this year?"

Randy reached for another piece of cake. "Sure, Mom. School is great. And I'm taking flying lessons. I want to learn to fly—like Dad. I've been studying flight rules and navigation this last semester."

"Hey, Randy, want me to put your truck in the garage?" Sis asked. Randy smiled and tossed her the ring of keys.

When Sis returned to the kitchen, she asked,

"What happened to your truck? The tail light is broken, and the bumper is dented."

Randy told them about the grey sedan and the driver with a ski mask. They both looked worried. Then he showed them Bill Markham's note. "Mom, did you tell anyone I was coming home today?"

Mrs. Flynn thought a moment. Then she said, "No, I didn't. But I was in the grocery store the other day. Bill Markham was there, too. I heard him telling some folks you had finished school for the summer and were coming home for a visit today. How did he know when you were coming, Randy?"

"I wrote him a note," Randy said. "I wanted to be sure he'd be in town when I got here."

"I also heard him say that you and he were going to prove that your father was not a thief." Mrs. Flynn's voice shook. Her eyes filled with tears. "Randy, it's been so long. Why not leave it alone?"

Randy took his plate and glass to the kitchen sink. "I can't, Mom. Things just don't add up. I know someone tried to scare me off the road today. That means someone must be worried that I'll find out the true story about Dad. Besides, I've got to find out what Bill Markham knows."

His mother put the pitcher of milk in the refrigerator. She turned to Randy. "It's hard to believe that someone was trying to hurt you. Couldn't it have just been some kid having fun? We're getting along fine now, Randy. You and Sis and I know that your father didn't steal. Why should we care what others think?"

"I do care, Mom," Randy said. "I'll always care. And deep down you care, too. Dad never even had a trial. And yet everybody in town is sure that he was a crook. I want to prove they are wrong. And Bill will help me. I told him I would meet him at Mule Deer Pass day after tomorrow."

"Good for you, Randy," Sis said. "Dad's name should be cleared. I'll help you any way I can."

That night Randy's dreams were filled with pheasants, planes, and a grey sedan. Its driver wore a brown ski mask.

Chapter 3

No Help at the Bank

Sunlight shot through the bedroom curtains like a laser beam. It was still cool in the morning. The birds chirped back and forth across the trees. Randy turned over on his back. It sounded as if someone were hammering on his door.

"Get up, lazybones," Sis yelled. "Breakfast is ready."

"OK, OK," Randy called. "I'm up, Sis." He rolled out of bed. What dreams, he thought. I feel as if I walked a thousand miles during the night. He dressed and went to the kitchen.

"What would you like for breakfast?" Mrs. Flynn asked. "I've got French toast and bacon on the stove."

"Thanks, Mom," Randy answered. "Nothing right now. I'll have a bite later on. I want to leave right away for the bank."

"The bank?" Mrs. Flynn asked. Both she and

Sis were staring at him. "Why are you going to the bank?"

"I want to see Ike Harper," Randy answered. "I want to ask him some questions."

"Be careful of what you say to him, Randy," Mrs. Flynn said. "He's been very nice to us. He didn't have to be, you know."

"Don't worry, Mom. I'll be polite." Randy gave her a big hug and left.

It was going to be a beautiful day. The morning sun felt warm on his back. The morning dew was cool and wet on his tennis shoes. The air was fresh and crisp. A beautiful day — and yet a dark, evil cloud hung over Randy. When he thought of Ski Mask and his father, somehow the day didn't seem so pretty. He decided to walk the five blocks to the bank.

"Randy, my boy!" Ike Harper called from his desk in a corner of the busy bank. "When did you get to town?"

"Good morning, Mr. Harper," Randy said. "I got in yesterday afternoon." Ike Harper is about the same size as Ski Mask, he thought. No, the short plump banker wasn't the type to play demolition derby.

"I heard you're back because of some crazy idea Bill Markham has," Mr. Harper said.

11

Randy grinned at him. "That's true. There sure aren't many secrets in this town."

Mr. Harper laughed, "You're right, Randy. The whole town knows Bill dragged you back here. Are you sure you want to dig up all that old business about your father?"

"Yes, I do," Randy said. "No one knows what really happened. I've got to find out the truth."

"Well, *I* know the truth," said a loud, harsh voice. Randy turned quickly.

"Oh, Randy," Mr. Harper said. "You remember Phil Stoner. He took your father's . . . your father's job. He's . . . He's the assistant manager now."

"I know," Randy said.

"Like I was saying, why put yourself through all of this?" Mr. Harper asked. "Why not let it be?"

"What Mr. Harper is saying," Stoner broke in, "is that it's a matter of record that your father owed $50,000 to that club in Reno. It's also a matter of record that when your father and the plane turned up missing, so did $50,000."

"You say this is all a matter of record." Randy did his best to sound polite. "But how come we didn't know that Dad was gambling? We would have known. At least my mother would have

known. But we didn't know a thing. And now we'll never know. The whole thing was dropped when the plane wasn't found. There wasn't even a trial."

"Trial?" Stoner was almost screaming. "What do you need, kid? The evidence we found speaks for itself." He glared at Randy.

Several people in the bank stopped and looked at them. Mr. Harper took out a handkerchief and mopped his forehead. Randy felt his cheeks grow red.

"I don't agree, Stoner," Randy said. "That evidence doesn't mean a thing to me because it doesn't make any sense. I want to find out the whole truth and nothing but the truth."

"Just be sure you can live with it, kid," Stoner said quietly.

"Oh, yeah? What's that supposed to mean?" Randy stepped closer to Stoner. His fists were clenched.

"Now, Randy," Mr. Harper broke in, "I'm sure Phil doesn't mean anything at all. You're home now. You have to do what you think is best. So go ahead. Find out the truth if you can. Just be sure you're man enough to live with it—whatever it is."

Chapter 4

Night Visitor

"So you see why I have to do this," Randy said. He had just finished reading Bill's letter to Sis and Mom. It was dark outside. A warm breeze was blowing. An owl hooted in the distance. The crickets sang to each other.

"But that letter doesn't tell us anything," Mrs. Flynn said. "What do you suppose Bill has found out there? And why is he keeping it a secret?"

"Who knows?" Randy asked. "But Bill Markham has been a good friend. He was always sure that Dad didn't do anything wrong."

"He's right. Dad *didn't* do anything wrong. I'm sure of it," Sis said. "The whole thing is just plain silly. If Dad had been gambling, we would have known it."

"I have always known your father was an honest man," Mrs. Flynn said. She picked up her knitting. "But you must admit that it did look

14

bad. First, he and the plane just vanished into thin air. Then the money was missing from the bank. I guess it all made sense to anyone who didn't know your father."

"And the I.O.U. from the gambling club in Reno," Randy added. "It was a real set-up."

"Mom, did Dad ever gamble?" Sis asked.

"Oh, sure," her mother answered. "Now and then he'd play a game of cards on a fishing trip. But that was all. $50,000 — never!"

"Then you understand why I've got to meet Bill up at Mule Deer Pass," Randy said. "It's now or never if we're going to clear Dad's name."

They sat there quietly. There was a lot to think about. All at once it seemed strangely quiet outside. They looked at one another.

"Gee, it seems quiet outside," Sis said. "It's kind of spooky. I don't even hear a cricket."

Randy said nothing. He put his fingers to his lips. "Shhh." He tiptoed to the screen door. He listened. Then he whispered, "There's someone outside. Just keep on talking as if everything were OK."

With a quick movement he flung the door open and leaped outside. He stood there a few moments. His eyes slowly got used to the darkness. He looked around the yard. Suddenly he spotted a dark figure. It was crouched near the garbage cans under the kitchen window. Could it be? Yes, it was. Ski Mask!

"Hey," Randy yelled. "Don't move. Freeze!" He started toward the figure, but he was too late. Ski Mask moved fast. He grabbed a garbage can and shoved it in front of Randy. Then he ran.

Randy fell over the garbage can. He lay there in a pile of orange peels, tin cans, and milk cartons. What a mess!

Mrs. Flynn and Sis had rushed out of the house at the sound of the crashing garbage can.

"Randy! Are you all right?" Mrs. Flynn looked pale in the moonlight. "What was it?"

"It was Ski Mask," Randy answered. He got up and brushed himself off. "I saw him, but he got away."

"You mean that turkey who ran into the Shiny Knight?" Sis asked.

"The same," Randy said. "And I almost had him."

"What could he have wanted?" Mrs. Flynn asked.

"I don't know," Randy answered. "But I aim to find out. Let's go inside. I'd like to wash this goop off."

Chapter 5

On Your Mark

The next day Randy knew he had to move fast. He didn't want any more trouble with Ski Mask. He had to buy food and supplies and head for the hills. He also wanted to be sure the Shiny Knight was in good shape. Nothing could go wrong. Meeting with Bill Markham at Mule Deer Pass was too important.

The food and supplies didn't cost too much. And it was a good thing. He was a little short of cash. Good old Sis had chipped in with some of her babysitting money. He bought mostly canned goods. They were heavy, but they would keep well on a three or four day trip.

One thing he didn't have to buy was binoculars. That morning Mrs. Flynn had handed him a leather case. "I've had your father's binoculars put away," she said. "Could you use them on this trip?"

"You bet, Mom," Randy smiled. "They will come in handy. I'll take real good care of them."

Randy stood outside the Calverton General Store loading the pick-up. He couldn't get the tailgate down. Not since Ski Mask had bumped the rear of the truck.

Mr. Harper was walking by. He stopped. "Doing some shopping, Randy?"

"Yes, Mr. Harper. Just a little." Randy didn't want to tell Mr. Harper any more than he already knew. That was the problem. The whole town seemed to know every move he made. "Are you on a coffee break or something?"

"Sometimes I like to get out of the bank for a breath of fresh air," Mr. Harper answered. He pointed to the supplies Randy was loading in the truck. "Going camping? Or does this have something to do with your father?"

"Mr. Harper," Randy said, "my father didn't steal the money from your bank. I'm going to prove it."

Mr. Harper put his hand on Randy's shoulder. "It seems to me that you should leave this kind of thing to the police. That's their job."

"I'd be glad to," Randy said, "if they would do anything. But they won't. As far as they are concerned, the case is closed."

"You may be right about that," said Mr. Harper. "But what if you find out after all that your father really did take the money?"

Randy was getting mad. "Look, he didn't take a red cent from the bank. But if it turns out that he did, well, OK. At least we'll know the truth at last."

"Well, Randy, I wish you the best of luck," Mr. Harper said. "Frankly, I don't think you're going to find a thing. You seem to trust that old coot Bill Markham. You're the only one in town who does."

"I sure do trust him," Randy said. "I've hunted with him. My father always said you learned an awful lot about a man when you hunted with him. Bill's the best."

"Well, maybe so," Mr. Harper said. "Say, what happened to the back of your truck?"

Randy put the last sack of supplies in the pick-up. "When I was driving into town, some nut in a ski mask tried to run me off the road."

"Probably some goofy kid," Mr. Harper said.

"If it was a kid, it sure was a strange one," Randy answered. "I saw the same guy sneaking around our house last night. I almost caught him, but he got away."

"This happened last night?" asked Mr.

Harper. He seemed surprised. He scratched his head. "And when did this guy try to run you off the road?"

"Like I said, when I first drove into town day before yesterday." Why was Mr. Harper asking all these questions, Randy wondered.

"During the afternoon?"

He scratched his head. "And when did this guy try to run you off the road?"

"Yep."

Mr. Harper seemed to lose interest. "Well, guess I better get back to the bank." He gave a nod to Randy as he turned to walk away. "You take it easy out there."

"Oh, you can count on that," Randy said under his breath. Had he told Mr. Harper too much? He watched the plump banker walk down the sidewalk toward the bank.

Phil Stoner stepped out of a doorway and caught up with Mr. Harper. The two men talked. Stoner laughed loudly and glanced back at Randy.

"They'll see," Randy said out loud. "They'll see." This guy Stoner was a real pain. And he had Dad's job. Suddenly a new thought struck Randy. Was it possible? Stoner was the same size as Ski Mask. He looked in good shape. He seemed light on his feet. Well, time will tell, Randy thought. It was getting late. He'd better head for home. He wanted to get an early start in the morning.

Chapter 6

Get Set!

"That dinner was great, Mom." Randy was drying the supper dishes. He placed the last plate in the cupboard. I've been home three days, and I've had three super dinners. You might get stuck with me!" He gave Mrs. Flynn a hug.

"Sis and I would love that, Randy," smiled his mother. "But I know that you'll have to go back to the city to finish school."

"Sure, but it wouldn't be so bad living here," Randy said. "After everything is cleared up."

"When and where are you going to meet Bill?" Sis asked.

Randy hung up the dish towel. "I'm taking the pick-up to King's Canyon tomorrow. I'll drive in just as far as I can get. Then I'll hike the rest of the way to Mule Deer Pass. Bill will be waiting for me day after tomorrow."

"What do you think he has found?" Sis asked.

22

"Has he ever given you a hint?"

"Nope," Randy answered. "Just that he found something that might clear Dad."

"Old Bill," Sis said. "I guess I've known him all my life. And I like him. But he is kind of a crazy old guy."

"Crazy like a fox," Randy grinned. "If he says he saw something up there that might help Dad, then he did. He knows the woods better than anyone else in these parts."

"Yes, he does," Mrs. Flynn agreed, "I was always glad when he went with you and your Dad on the hunting trips. I knew I didn't have to worry about your getting lost. How long do you plan on being out there, Randy?"

"Three or four days at most, Mom."

His mother finished setting the table for breakfast. "What time are you planning to leave in the morning? I want to fix you a big breakfast before you start the trip. It may be your last hot food for a while."

"Don't bother, Mom," Randy said. "I'm going to leave before the sun comes up. In fact, since I'll be leaving so early, I'll say goodbye now and go to bed."

"Be careful, Randy," his mother said.

"I will," said Randy as he left the room.

"What do you think they'll find, Mom?" Sis asked.

"I don't really know," answered Mrs. Flynn. "But Randy is right to trust Bill Markham. He's a fine man. And Randy is like his father. Once he makes up his mind to do something, there's no stopping him. They'll find something."

Sis looked at her mother. "I sure hope they do. It's been almost four years since Dad went away. The kids at school still say things now and then. I know they don't mean to hurt my feelings, but they do."

Mrs. Flynn had just turned off the kitchen lights when they heard a loud explosion. It shook the small house.

"What the . . . ?" Sis yelled.

"Come on!" Mrs. Flynn ran toward the living room window. The whole yard in front of the house was lit up in a bright orange glow.

"What was that?" Randy yelled. He streaked from his bedroom in his pajamas. He raced over to the big picture window. "Oh, no," he groaned. "No!"

"What is it?" His mother and sister asked at the same time. Then they saw it. The Shiny Knight was covered in flames. They could hear the fire crackle. They could smell the smoke.

Firebombed! They just stood there.

Then they heard the brass bell calling the Volunteer Fire Department. And then the shrill sound of the siren on the hook and ladder truck as it sped towards them.

Flames rose eight feet in the air. In just a few minutes the Shiny Knight was a lump of twisted, steaming metal.

Then they saw it. The Shiny Knight was covered in flames.

Chapter 7

Go!

"Thanks for driving me this far, Sis," Randy said. They were on an old logging road. It ended at King's Canyon. The old family station wagon rolled and pitched like a ship on the high seas.

"I don't mind at all, Randy," Sis answered. "This trip is important to all of us."

Randy hadn't slept much the night before. It was hard to believe the Shiny Knight was gone. He didn't know when he would be able to get another pick-up. He needed every penny for school.

He couldn't put off the trip. He might miss Bill. Also, there was no telling what Ski Mask might do next. He was sure his mother and sister would be OK. Ski Mask was after him, nobody else.

Randy pointed to a wide spot in the road. "You can pull over and let me out there. If we try to go any further, we'll beat this old wagon to death."

"Are you sure this is close enough?" Sis asked. "I thought you were going to drive all the way to Lost Lake Trail. That's a long way off."

"This station wagon can't get that far," Randy answered. "We'd bust the crank case for sure."

"But you'll never make Mule Deer Pass today," Sis said.

"Can't be helped," said her brother. "You just turn this thing around and get home. You know Mom will worry if you're not back for breakfast. Tell her everything is going to be all right."

Sis backed the old car up and turned it around. She started back down the trail. A cloud of dust rose in back of the station wagon like a rooster tail.

Randy looked around. It was just getting light. The sun was peeping over the top of the canyon. A jack rabbit hopped into the middle of the road. It sat there sniffing the air. Then it hopped off the road on the other side.

Looks like it's going to be a good day, Randy thought. Too bad he didn't have the pick-up. He could have driven farther and saved time. Now he would never make Mule Deer Pass today. With luck maybe some time late tomorrow morning. He hoped Bill would wait for him.

"Well, I better get started," he said aloud. He threw his pack frame on his back. It was a long walk to the cut-off to Lost Lake Trail. He would have to ration his food. He started up the trail.

He had been walking for almost five hours. He couldn't shake the feeling that someone or something was following him. It was a creepy feeling—like a cold wind blowing on the back of his neck. He didn't like the feeling at all.

Now and then he stepped off the trail and hid in some brush. He sat there without moving for ten minutes. Nothing. The birds sang. The high wind blew in the tree tops. Mosquitoes bit him. But nothing else. Just the sounds of the forest. No footsteps. No voices. No sound of someone hiking up the road behind him.

Then he would step back on the trail sure that no one was close by. But still he couldn't shake that spooky feeling. If someone is following me, he thought, he can't be very close.

Finally he decided to settle it once and for all. He'd wait until he got to the cut-off to Lost Lake Trail. He'd climb up on some jagged rock. From there he could see all of King's Canyon below him. Dad's binoculars will sure come in handy, he thought. I'm glad Mom thought of giving them to me.

As Randy hiked on, he tried to get his thoughts in order. It made sense that someone would be following him. Why not? Ski Mask had tried to run him off the road. And Ski Mask had been prowling around the house. And he was sure it was Ski Mask who had burned the Shiny Knight. Why would he stop now?

Finally he came to the cut-off to Lost Lake Trail. He slipped his pack off and climbed out on a rocky ledge. He lay down on a flat rock and took out the binoculars. Slowly he scanned the path he had just walked.

"Well, I'll be darned," he said softly. "I knew it!" Somebody *was* following him. The figure was almost two miles back. It walked slowly and then stopped. He's studying the trail to see if I've been that way, Randy thought. The figure was too far away for Randy to tell who it was—even with binoculars. But he could tell it was a young man. Maybe a little older than Randy. He was carrying a pack on his back.

Gosh, I hope Sis didn't bump into that guy, he thought. Why didn't I bring Dad's gun?

Chapter 8

Shots in the Dark

It was dark. The stars looked like gold buttons on dark blue cloth. Not a cloud in the sky. Randy sat by his campfire. He felt full and sleepy. The pork and beans had tasted great. His father had taught him how to heat a can of beans over an open fire. Just tie a green stick to the can for a handle. Then it was easy to lift the can on and off the fire. And coffee always tasted better when it was cooked slowly over a campfire.

He wished his father were there. Those were great days, he thought. He threw the rest of his coffee on the fire. Time to turn in and try to get some sleep. He had to get an early start in the morning. Then he might be able to get to Mule Deer Pass in time to meet Bill Markham.

He had already made his plans for the night. He unrolled his sleeping bag. He put it in the shadows near the small fire. Then he stuffed a blanket and some supplies into the bag. He stepped back and looked at it. Yes, it looked like someone was asleep in the bag. He picked up another blanket and wrapped it around himself Indian-style. Then he crawled into some bushes next to a big rock. It felt good to be taking some action against Ski Mask. It made him feel in control. He had been feeling like a target for days, and he didn't like it. Now it was his turn. He felt like a man.

Even so, Randy thought, I wish I had Dad's gun. Yet it had seemed like a good idea to leave it at home for Mom and Sis. Just in case Ski Mask decided to pay them another visit.

Well, anyway, if Ski Mask was following him, that meant Mom and Sis were OK. And Ski Mask wasn't going to catch him off guard. Not this time.

Randy didn't have long to wait. The flames from the small fire had died down to coals. The forest was as quiet as a graveyard. He was beginning to doze off.

Then he heard the sound of something crackling in the bush. Something that was walking on two legs toward the camp site.

Randy moved closer to the big rock. He was careful not to make a sound. I hope that guy doesn't spot me, he thought. But I don't have time to move farther away. The sound of snapping twigs and footsteps came closer. He could hear the man breathing heavily. He must have stumbled. Randy could hear him swear. Whoever was out there wasn't used to the woods. Tough luck, old buddy, Randy thought.

Then there was silence. The dark figure had reached the camp site. It stood there without moving. Randy peeked from behind his hiding place. Ski Mask! Then he heard a click he knew well. It was a safety lever coming off an automatic pistol. Even though it was chilly in the mountains at night, Randy was covered with sweat.

BANG! BANG! BANG! BANG! Four shots rang out, one after another. It sounded like an Army 45. The echo from the shots bounced all over the forest. Ski Mask ran up to the sleeping bag. His pistol was pointed, ready to fire again. He kicked the sleeping bag.

"Blast it!" Ski Mask yelled. He knew he had been tricked. He looked around quickly. His pistol was still drawn. Then he rushed from the camp site. Randy heard him charging through the brush like a wounded bear.

Chapter 9

Flight

At first light everything was covered with a thin layer of frost. Randy shivered in his blanket. At first he couldn't get to sleep after the shooting. After about an hour he settled down. I've got to get some sleep, he thought. I've got to have a clear head tomorrow.

He carefully looked out from his hiding place next to the rock. The camp site looked empty. The stuffed sleeping bag had four ragged bullet holes in it.

"I guess it really did happen," he said to himself. Somehow it was hard to believe that a man out there really meant to kill him. Again he looked over the camp site carefully. He wasn't going to make a move until he was sure no one was hiding in the bushes.

Finally he was sure that no one was lying in wait. He stood up slowly. Every joint in his body ached. But at least he was alive!

Randy knew he needed a weapon. He couldn't fight the guy with his bare hands. Didn't Bill Markham usually carry both a rifle and a pistol? Yes, he did. Randy was sure of it. Well, he had better get to Bill. Fast!

It would take him about three hours to get to Mule Deer Pass. Maybe two and a half hours if he ran. Or should he just head home and give it all up? No! He had come this far. He had to finish what he had started. He took off up Lost Lake Trail at a dead run.

He ran as he had never run before. He used strength he didn't know he had. His feet pounded up the trail. His breath came in painful gasps. His clothes were soaked in sweat.

The trail reached a level spot. Running wasn't quite so hard now. He ran on. Finally he knew he had to stop and rest. He sat down and waited for his heart to stop pounding. He listened. He heard no one. Did Ski Mask change his mind? Did he go back to Calverton?

"No way," Randy said out loud. "He's out there. I feel it." He got up and started to run again. A branch on the trail slapped across his face. The sharp pain brought tears to his eyes.

Suddenly one ankle gave way, and he went

down with a mighty thud. He lay there and rubbed the ankle. He tasted blood in his mouth where the branch had cut his lips.

Somehow he got to his feet again and started running. He played games with himself as he made his way up the rough path. Anything to forget how tired he was. For a little while he pretended he was a quarterback making a 90 yard punt return. Then he tried counting his steps. His legs pumped up the trail.

"A long trip begins with a single step," he mumbled. "296, 297, 298 . . . " Then, at last, there was Mule Deer Pass in front of him. But where was Bill?

"Hold it right there, kid," a loud voice called. Randy stopped. Ski Mask stepped out of the bushes. The 45 pistol in his hand looked huge. Its big barrel was pointed right at Randy's chest.

Randy tried to catch his breath. "I know who you are," he panted. "I know your voice."

"We'll just skip the small talk, kid," Ski Mask answered. "Step over here next to this tree. Come on. Hurry up! Get a move on!"

Randy moved as slowly as he dared. "You'll never get away with this. They'll find out."

"Sure, kid," Ski Mask said. "And crime does not pay. So what else is new?"

"You've got to be crazy," Randy said. "You stole that money. You had something to do with what happened to my father. And now you think you're going to kill me. It'll never work."

"You're wrong, buddy," Ski Mask grinned. "It's worked for four years. It's going to keep on working. You just say your prayers, kid." He stepped back from Randy. He pointed the big gun at Randy's heart. Then he cocked the hammer.

"You kill that boy, and I won't kill you," a crusty old voice yelled from the bushes. "But you'll just wish I did!" Ski Mask froze. Then he threw down his gun. It was all over.

Randy's legs suddenly felt weak. He sat down and leaned against the tree. "Bill, you're a sight for sore eyes. That was too close for comfort. Am I glad to see you!"

"You know this guy?" Bill asked. "I think I've heard that voice before." He yanked off the ski mask.

"Stoner," Randy said. "I knew it was you." There was no surprise in his voice.

"You'll never prove anything," Stoner growled. "It's just your word against mine. The word of the son of a thief. And nobody will believe this crazy old coot either."

"You took that money, Stoner," Randy said. "I know you did."

"Prove it, kid. Everyone thinks your father took that money. They always will," Stoner answered.

"No, they won't," said Bill. "Here Randy. Tie his hands behind his back. Then I've got

Ski Mask froze. Then he threw down his gun. It was all over.

something to show you."

Randy tied Stoner's wrists tightly. Then he turned to Bill. "You found the plane, Bill?"

"Up there." Bill pointed towards the hill. "I been here since early yesterday. Been clearing brush and such. Come on. I'll show you."

The three men walked up the hill. Bill first, then Stoner, then Randy. When they reached the top, Randy saw it. The wreckage of a blue and white plane.

"Look over here, Randy," Bill said. He pointed to the sandy bank of a small creek. "Tell me what you see." Randy got down on his hands and knees. He stuck his fingers into the sticky sand.

"Why, it's oil," he said in surprise.

"That's right," Bill answered. "Oil just don't sit on the side of a creek bed next to a berry patch. Not unless there's something that uses oil inside that old patch."

"Something like a wrecked plane," Randy said slowly. "You really put two and two together, Bill. Good for you."

"Not that good," Bill answered. "I must have walked by that creek seven or eight times. I missed that oil every single time. Guess it's been leaking out of the plane for a long time."

Randy looked him straight in the eye. "What about Dad, Bill? Is he in there?"

Suddenly Bill looked sad and tired and old. "Yes, he is Randy." He put his shabby old arm around Randy's shoulders. "Do you want to see him?"

Randy stood very still for a moment. "Yes," he said softly. "I guess I do."

They tied Stoner tightly to a pine tree. Then they walked over to the wreck. Randy pulled himself up on a broken wing. He looked inside the cockpit. A skeleton lay across the front seats. On its arm was a gold watch.

Randy looked down at Bill. "It's Dad," he said softly. "That's the watch Mom gave him for his birthday. I'd know it anywhere." He climbed down off the wreck.

"I know, Randy," Bill said. "I'm used to the idea now. You'll get used to it, too, in time. And I'll tell you something that will make you feel lots better. I've been over every inch of that plane. No luggage, no money, no passport, not even a heavy coat! Your father wasn't running away. He wasn't a thief!"

Chapter 10

Homecoming

When he finally got home, Randy slept for 16 hours. The last few days were a blur. He was worn out.

Bill had left him at the crash site with food, blankets, and a rifle. Randy's ankle was so swollen, he couldn't walk back. Bill marched Stoner back to Calverton and turned him over to the police chief. The next day a helicopter flew in and lifted Randy off the hill. At the same time some government men came to town to see what they could learn about the plane crash.

The door to Randy's bedroom opened a crack. Sis peeked into the room.

"Here you go, hero," she grinned. She brought in a tray and put it on Randy's lap. Mrs. Flynn followed her through the door.

Randy looked at his mother. "How are you and Sis, Mother? We know that Dad won't be coming home. Can you handle that?"

"I knew four years ago that he wasn't coming back, Randy," Mrs. Flynn said. "I knew that if he was alive, he would have come back to us somehow."

"You've got a visitor, Randy," Sis said.

"Bill?" he asked.

"No, Mr. Harper." Sis left the room and came back quickly with Ike Harper.

"Well, you did it, son," Harper said. They shook hands.

"I just wanted to stop by and say a few things, Randy." The banker tugged at his tie to straighten it. "First of all, we're going to hold a special service in honor of your father."

"I'm glad to hear that," Randy said. "Dad deserves that from the town."

"There's more," said Mr. Harper. "The bank is going to give a reward to your family. I don't know how much yet. But it should help out quite a bit. Also, your father had a pension coming to him. We couldn't give it to your mother before but we can now."

"Thanks, Mr. Harper," Randy said. "What about Stoner. Did he confess?"

"He sure did," Harper grinned. "And it didn't take long. Not once all the facts were in."

"But how?" Randy asked. "Up on the mountain he was sure he'd get out of it."

"Things just began to add up," said Mr. Harper. "Remember that day we talked in front of the store? I remembered then that Stoner had taken the day off the day you drove into town. And the night you almost caught him outside your house—well, I called him that night to ask about a bank matter. And he wasn't home."

"So you began to suspect Stoner then?" Randy asked.

"Yes," Harper went on. "The next thing I did was hop a flight to Reno. I went to see the manager of that gambling club. I showed him a picture of your Dad and one of Stoner."

"And that was that," Mrs. Flynn broke in. Her eyes were sparkling. "The manager pointed to Stoner's picture right away. He had never laid eyes on your father. Didn't know him at all!"

"There's more," Mr. Harper said. "When Stoner called in and asked for a few days off on the same day you left, I was pretty sure he was going after you. That was when I called the police."

"They went right over to Stoner's house, but they were too late. He had already left," Sis said.

"There's one more thing," Randy said. "What

about Dad? What was he doing up in that plane? Why didn't he tell anyone where he was going?"

"We're still not sure about that, Randy," said Mr. Harper. "But we've got a few ideas. We think your father may have suspected Stoner of taking money from the bank. He knew Stoner was a gambler. He may have been on his way to Reno to dig up a few facts."

"But what about the crash?" Randy asked.

Mr. Harper pushed his glasses up on his nose. "We don't know about that either. Maybe it was just plain engine trouble. Maybe Stoner knew what your father was planning and did something to the plane. I'm sure the government men will find some answers in a few days."

"Well, that's that," said Randy. "It's good to have it all behind us. Thank you for coming over and telling us, Mr. Harper."

"There's more, hero," Sis grinned.

Mr. Harper had a big smile on his face. The biggest Randy had ever seen. He reached in his coat pocket. "This is for you," he said. He handed Randy a set of keys.

Randy looked at them. "It can't be," he said. "I've got to see this!" He hopped out of bed. His mother handed him his crutches.

They all walked into the living room. Randy

looked out the picture window. His eyes grew wide. A dark blue pick-up with chrome wheels was parked in front of the house. On the side of the truck in large white letters were the words: Shiny Knight II.

"This is for you," he said. He handed Randy a set of keys.